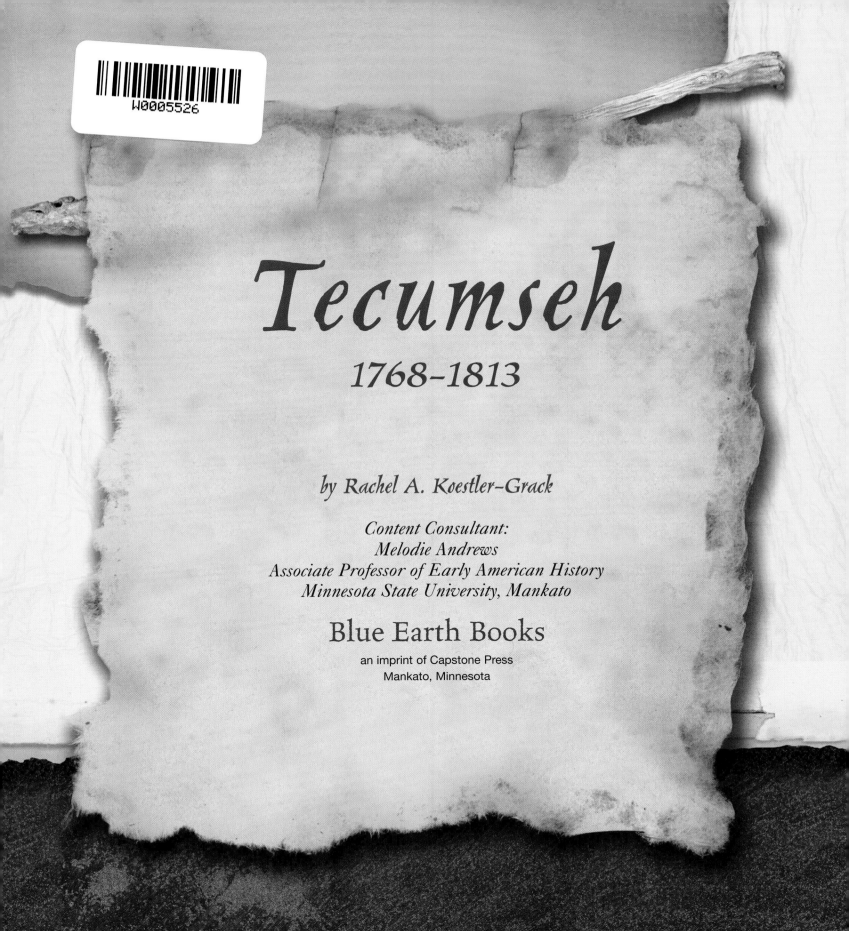

Tecumseh

1768–1813

by Rachel A. Koestler-Grack

Content Consultant:
Melodie Andrews
Associate Professor of Early American History
Minnesota State University, Mankato

Blue Earth Books

an imprint of Capstone Press
Mankato, Minnesota

Blue Earth Books are published by Capstone Press
151 Good Counsel Drive, P.O. Box 669, Mankato, Minnesota 56002
http://www.capstone-press.com

Library of Congress Cataloging-in-Publication Data
Koestler-Grack, Rachel A., 1973–
     Tecumseh, 1768–1813 / by Rachel A. Koestler-Grack.
     p. cm. — (American Indian biographies)
     Includes bibliographical references (p. 31) and index.
     Summary: A biography of the Shawnee leader who united a confederacy of Indians in an effort to
save Indian land from the advance of white soldiers and settlers.
     ISBN 0-7368-1212-1 (hardcover)
     1. Tecumseh, Shawnee chief, 1768–1813—Juvenile literature. 2. Shawnee Indians—Biography—
Juvenile literature. 3. Shawnee Indians—History—Juvenile literature. [1. Tecumseh, Shawnee Chief, 1768–1813.
2. Shawnee Indians—Biography. 3. Indians of North America—Biography. 4. Kings, queens, rulers, etc.] I. Title.
II. Series.
     E99.S35 T164 2003
     977.004'973'0092—dc21   2001006472

Editorial credits
Editor: Megan Schoeneberger
Cover Designer: Heather Kindseth
Interior Layout Designers: Jennifer Schonborn
     and Heather Kindseth
Interior Illustrator: Jennifer Schonborn
Production Designers: Jennifer Schonborn
     and Gene Bentdahl
Photo Researcher: Mary Englar

Photo credits
Paramount Press/Robert Griffing, cover, 4–5, 29
(bottom); Ohio Historical Society, cover
(tomahawk); Portsmouth Murals Inc./Robert
Dafford, 8–9; Geoffrey Harding, 11, 14; Gray
Stone Press/David Wright, 13; Capstone
Press/Gary Sundermeyer, 15, 25; Corbis, 16–17,
24, 26; Art Resource, 19; North Wind Picture
Archives, 20; Detroit Institute of Arts (negative:
CP-186; CIS 2292), 21; Library of Congress, 22,
29 (top); Hulton/Archive by Getty Images, 28

Contents

CHAPTER 1
A Vision of Unity

Tecumseh (center) and his Shawnee people lived in the Ohio Valley for many years. He dedicated his life to protecting Shawnee lands and the Shawnee way of life.

In late summer 1810, Tecumseh stood on a rock ridge near the Wabash River in present-day Indiana. Below him was the beginning of his great vision, a united Indian confederacy. Between 1807 and 1810, Tecumseh united about 500 warriors of several American Indian tribes in one village.

He looked down at Tippecanoe Village, or Prophet's Town, with a sense of hope. In the village, warriors were busy making weapons. Tecumseh's brother Temskwautawa was a religious leader also known as The Prophet. He encouraged the warriors. He reminded them that they must protect their traditional way of life. He also told them that it was their responsibility to protect the land the Great Spirit had given to them.

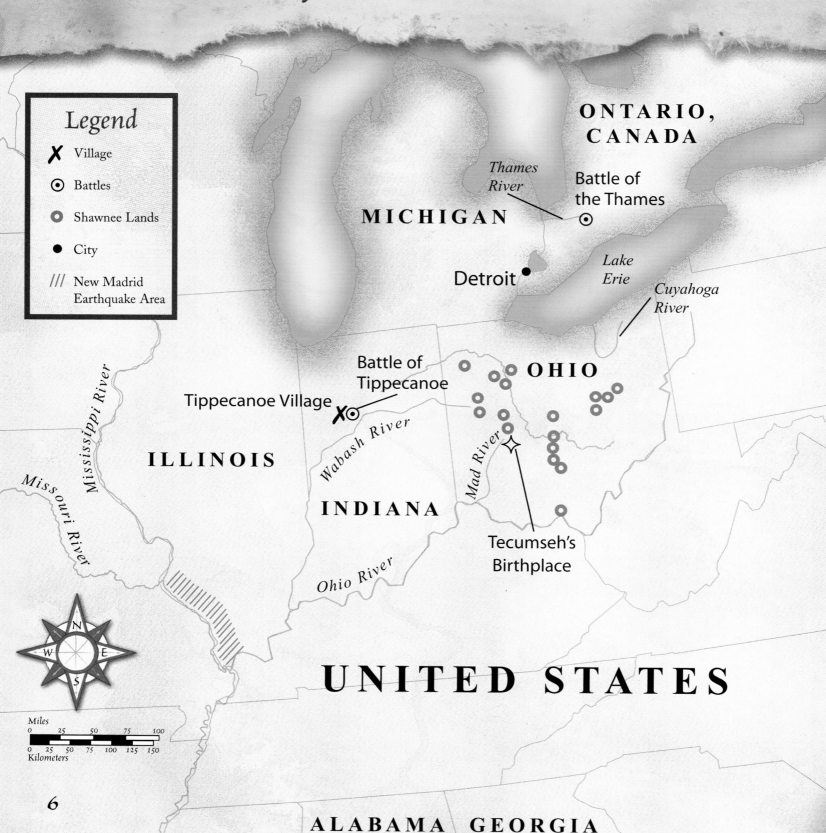

Tecumseh's Territory

Legend

X Village
⊙ Battles
◎ Shawnee Lands
● City
/// New Madrid Earthquake Area

ONTARIO, CANADA

Thames River

Battle of the Thames ⊙

MICHIGAN

Lake Erie

Detroit ●

Cuyahoga River

OHIO

Battle of Tippecanoe

Tippecanoe Village X⊙

Wabash River

ILLINOIS

Mississippi River

Missouri River

Mad River

INDIANA

Ohio River

Tecumseh's Birthplace

UNITED STATES

N
W E
S

Miles
0 25 50 75 100

Kilometers
0 25 50 75 100 125 150

ALABAMA GEORGIA

In the late 1700s when Tecumseh was a young man, white settlers began settling lands beyond what was then the western border of the United States. White people wanted to live on and farm land in the Ohio Valley. This land belonged to the Shawnee. When white people tried to buy the land, the Shawnee people refused to sell it.

Instead of respecting this decision, white leaders forced the Shawnee off their land. White settlers continued to push Tecumseh's people further west into Indiana.

As Tecumseh grew older, he realized that something must be done to protect the Shawnee way of life. The Shawnee had lost much of their hunting grounds to white settlers. With less land, they were not free to travel and hunt as their ancestors had done. Tecumseh believed that if all American Indians joined together as one nation, the white people would respect their wishes and let them live in peace.

Prophet's Town was still small. But Tecumseh hoped it would grow strong. As soon as the leaves began to change colors, he planned to travel south to Alabama and Georgia. There, he would visit the villages of his mother's people, the Creek Indians. He hoped to convince these native groups to join his confederacy.

Tecumseh never gave up hope for a united Indian nation. He believed that in time the Great Spirit would lead the tribes to see that they needed each other. Together, they would be strong enough to protect their lands. Today, people recognize Tecumseh for his efforts to make peace with the white people and protect the American Indian way of life.

CHAPTER 2
Panther across the Sky

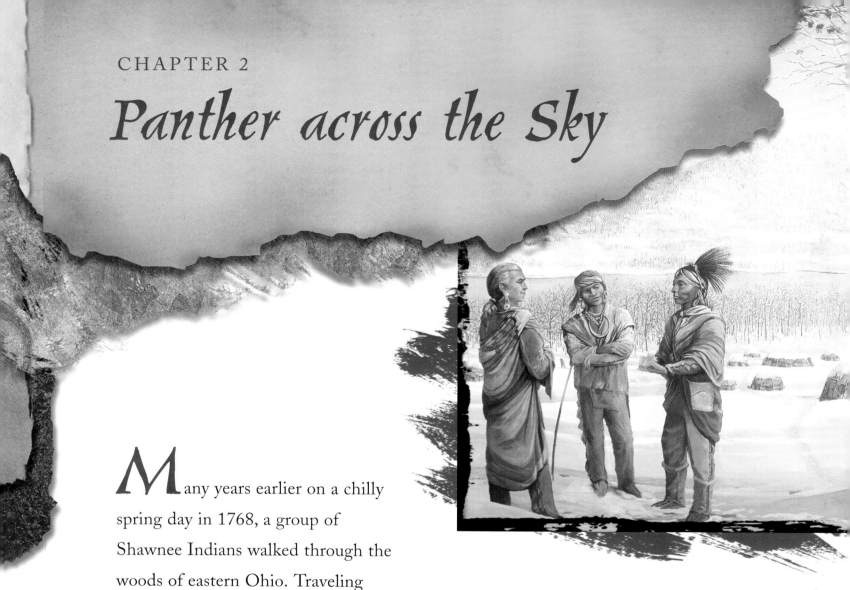

Many years earlier on a chilly spring day in 1768, a group of Shawnee Indians walked through the woods of eastern Ohio. Traveling with the group were Tecumseh's father and mother, Pucksinwah and Methotasa. The group was on its way to a great Shawnee council.

As evening approached, Pucksinwah often checked on his wife. She was in labor and would have her baby soon. Just miles from the council village, Methotasa had to stop. It was time for the baby to be born.

Pucksinwah told the Shawnee leaders to continue without them. He called to his oldest son and daughter who were playing with the other Shawnee children. A few Shawnee women stayed with the family to help deliver the baby.

*When Tecumseh was a boy, he lived in a
Shawnee village in the Ohio Valley.*

Pucksinwah helped the women build a shelter for Methotasa near the Mad
River. He told his 12-year-old son, "Chiksika, go gather firewood." His daughter,
Tecumapease, cared for her younger brother, Sauwaseekau.

Outside the shelter, Pucksinwah and Chiksika patiently waited for one of the
women to announce the baby's birth. Pucksinwah wrapped a blanket tightly around
his shoulders and watched the puffs of his breath vanish into the dark night air.

While Pucksinwah and Chiksika were staring into the night, a shooting star glittered across the black sky. Chiksika looked at his father in wonder, remembering the stories he had heard the elders tell many times. According to Shawnee elders, the shooting star was The Panther, a powerful spirit, who passed across the sky each night. Very rarely did the spirit show itself to people.

A moment after the star vanished, Pucksinwah and Chiksika heard the burst of a baby's cry from inside the shelter. A Shawnee woman stepped out from behind the deer hide door. "You have a son," she said.

Pucksinwah told Methotasa about the shooting star. They both agreed this event was a sign from the Great Spirit. They named the boy Tecumseh, which means "the panther passing across."

Tecumseh grew up in his Ohio village as a typical Shawnee boy. In addition to his sister and two older brothers, Tecumseh had three younger brothers. Tecumseh was especially fond of Chiksika and Tecumapease.

Tecumseh played games that improved his skills as a hunter and warrior. He practiced shooting arrows at rolling hoops to improve his accuracy. During winter, Tecumseh wrestled in the snow with other Shawnee boys to strengthen his muscles. Tecumseh fought in pretend battles with his friends. Oftentimes, Tecumseh was the leader, testing battle strategies.

When Tecumseh was 7 years old, his father was killed in a battle with the white people. The village chief did not have any sons and took special interest in Tecumseh. He noticed Tecumseh's skill as a leader among the other Shawnee boys. Because Tecumseh lost his father, the Shawnee chief spent much time teaching Tecumseh about traditional Shawnee ways. Chiksika also looked after Tecumseh. Chiksika was a respected and brave warrior. He taught his skills to Tecumseh.

Like other northeastern American Indians, older members of the tribe taught boys traditional ways. Chiksika taught Tecumseh after their father's death.

After the death of Pucksinwah, Tecumseh's mother returned to her native Creek village in Alabama. The children stayed with the Shawnee people. Tecumapease took care of her younger brothers after Methotasa left.

CHAPTER 3

Growing Up Shawnee

Like other Shawnee men, Tecumseh enjoyed hunting in his people's native lands.

Tecumseh began training to be a warrior at age 8. During his training, Tecumseh painted his face black. The black paint reminded Tecumseh of his serious role as a Shawnee warrior. The village elders then sent Tecumseh into a nearby woods to sit alone for several hours. Tecumseh did not eat during this time. This time alone would teach Tecumseh to concentrate. As Tecumseh grew older, his time of fasting increased, until he sat alone and without food for an entire day.

At about age 14, Tecumseh joined a war party led by Chiksika. Tecumseh had never watched warriors in battle, and he was scared. When he remembered the battle in later years, he said, "It was the only time in my life I felt afraid. When I heard the war whoops and saw the blood, I ran and hid beside a log."

Tecumseh enjoyed spending time hunting. He proved to be a skilled hunter. After returning from hunting expeditions, Tecumseh often showed his generosity and compassion by giving his kill to the elderly and sick people of his village.

In the late 1700s, white settlers began moving onto American Indian land. Many tribes were willing to share their land. But whites often settled American Indian land without permission. This disregard angered many American Indian groups.

In 1787, Tecumseh went with Chiksika on a hunting party. The group traveled west into present-day Illinois.

During their trip, they joined a Cherokee war party. The Cherokee Indians planned to attack a U.S. fort.

Before the attack, Chiksika had a vision that he would be killed during the battle. He told Tecumseh that he would be shot and killed in the fight. Tecumseh desperately tried to convince Chiksika not to fight. But Chiksika was determined to be a brave warrior.

As Chiksika foretold, he was killed during the battle. At the sight of the brave warrior falling to the ground, the other warriors panicked and retreated. The group of Shawnee Indians then traveled back to their home villages. During their return trip, Tecumseh grieved the loss of his brother.

As a young man, Tecumseh proved to have strong skills as a warrior. He quickly gained the respect of other Shawnee warriors.

14

Shawnee Blackberry Pudding

Shawnee Indians made blackberry pudding for special ceremonies and celebrations. Tecumapease probably made blackberry pudding in celebration of Tecumseh's successful hunts.

What You Need

Ingredients

⅓ cup (75 mL) butter

2 cups (500 mL) sugar, divided

2 cups (500 mL) flour

2 teaspoons (10 mL) baking powder

1 cup (250 mL) milk

1 tablespoon (15 mL) butter, for greasing

2 cups (500 mL) frozen blackberries, thawed

2 cups (500 mL) boiling water

Equipment

electric mixer

dry-ingredient measuring cups

large mixing bowl

liquid measuring cup

measuring spoons

paper towel

2-quart (2-liter) baking dish

wooden spoon

small saucepan

What You Do

1. Preheat the oven to 350°F (180°C).
2. Use electric mixer to cream together butter and 1 cup (250 mL) sugar in the large bowl.
3. Add flour, baking powder, and milk. Mix well.
4. Use paper towel dabbed with butter to lightly grease the baking dish.
5. Fold dough into the baking dish, patting it to cover the bottom of the dish.
6. Pour blackberries on top of dough mixture.
7. Sprinkle 1 cup (250 mL) sugar over the top of the blackberries.
8. Bring water to a boil over high heat. Immediately pour the boiling water over the blackberries.
9. Place baking dish in the oven.
10. Bake for about 50 minutes or until top is golden brown. Let pudding cool before serving.

Makes 8 to 10 servings

CHAPTER 4

The Rise and Fall of Tippecanoe

The Prophet led the warriors at Tippecanoe Village into battle against the U.S. Army. The warriors were quickly defeated.

By 1795, Tecumseh had become a war chief and civil leader of his people. He began his own village near Buck Creek in Ohio. His village was made up of about 250 Shawnee people.

In 1795, many American Indian groups of the Northeast signed a peace treaty with the United States. In the treaty, the tribes agreed to give up their claims to the northern part of Ohio, near Lake Erie. In return, the American Indians could have the land south of the Great Lakes, east of the Mississippi River, north of the Ohio River, and south of the Cuyahoga River. This land included much of Ohio, Indiana, and Illinois. White officials told the American Indians this treaty would last "as long as the woods grow and waters run." But they soon pushed American Indians off this land as well.

Tecumseh did not sign this treaty. To Tecumseh, land could not be bought or sold. He believed the Great Spirit had given his people the land to use, not to own and sell. Instead, he wanted freedom for his people to live and to hunt as the Shawnee Indians had always done.

To keep peace with the white settlers, Tecumseh moved his village within the treaty boundaries. He built Tippecanoe Village in western Indiana near the Wabash River. He began to talk with other Shawnee leaders about creating an Indian confederacy. By joining as one nation, Tecumseh hoped the American Indians could protect their lands and cultures.

Tecumseh's younger brother, Temskwautawa, was a powerful spiritual leader among the Shawnee people. People sometimes called him The Prophet. The Prophet strongly believed the Shawnee should hold on to their traditional ways of life. He helped Tecumseh convince American Indian groups to join the confederacy.

In the fall of 1810, Tecumseh traveled throughout the South, visiting with American Indian tribes. He told them about his vision of a great Indian confederacy. Many native tribes agreed to join the confederacy. He gave each group a special prayer stick. Special symbols had been carved into the stick. A symbol near the top of the stick represented an earthquake. At this final sign, all warriors should travel north to Tippecanoe Village.

In November 1811, Tecumseh was away, and the U.S. Army crossed into Shawnee territory. Although Tecumseh told his brother to keep peace with the whites, The Prophet rallied the warriors at Tippecanoe Village to fight. He told the warriors that he had a vision that they would win.

The warriors attacked the white soldiers early in the morning, hoping to take the soldiers by surprise. But the army was prepared to fight. Without Tecumseh to lead them, the warriors were unorganized and began to retreat. Within two hours, Tecumseh's warriors were defeated.

After the battle, many of the warriors returned to their home villages. The white soldiers destroyed Tippecanoe Village. Two of Tecumseh's friends got on their horses and rode south to find Tecumseh and tell him the bad news. Tecumseh gained support from some southern tribes and was pleased with his trip. When he heard about his brother's foolishness, he was angry. After the Battle of Tippecanoe, Tecumseh did not trust his brother for help and advice.

The Prophet, a powerful spiritual leader among the Shawnee, convinced the Shawnee to fight to keep their traditional way of life.

*Tecumseh was angry at his brother for disobeying
his orders to keep peace with the whites.*

On December 16, 1811, the signal on Tecumseh's prayer stick came true. A great
earthquake shook the ground in the early morning hours, swallowing large chunks of
land. The earthquake struck near New Madrid, Illinois, where the Ohio River and the
Missouri River meet the Mississippi River. This sign meant the southern tribes should
travel north to Tecumseh's village.

Shawnee Prayer Stick

When Tecumseh visited the southern tribes, he gave each tribal chief a prayer stick. This red cedar board had symbols and secret messages carved into it. The sticks were intended to unite all American Indian tribes by encouraging the chiefs to protect their culture. Tecumseh tied each prayer stick in a bundle of red-dyed sticks. Each stick represented a moon, or a month. Tecumseh told the chiefs to throw one stick away at each full moon, until only one stick remained. The chiefs should then watch the sky for Tecumseh's sign, which was a shooting star. When they saw this sign, they were to cut the last stick into 30 pieces, and burn one piece each night. When the last piece burned in the fire, a great trembling of the earth was supposed to occur.

CHAPTER 5

Joining the British

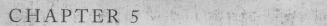

Tecumseh wanted freedom for American Indians to continue living their traditional way of life.

After the warriors' defeat at the Battle of Tippecanoe, Tecumseh lost the support of some tribes. Tecumseh tried to come to a peace agreement with white officials. But the U.S. government wanted Tecumseh and his people to give up their homelands in Ohio and Indiana. Tecumseh simply wanted freedom for the American Indians to live in peace.

During the early 1800s, relations between the United States and Great Britain became strained. In 1812, the United States declared war against Great Britain. In addition to other conflicts, the U.S. government hoped to obtain land owned by Great Britain in the northern part of North America. If the U.S. Army defeated the British, the land would become property of the United States. American Indians lived on this land.

British officials promised to let the American Indians keep their lands if they fought for the British army. Tecumseh believed this solution was the only way his people would be able to keep their freedom. He tried to convince other American Indian groups to join the British. Some American Indian groups joined Tecumseh. Others fought for the U.S. Army.

"... Where today are the Pequot? Where today are the Narrangansett, the Mohican, the Pakanoket, and many other once powerful tribes of our people? They have vanished before the avarice [greed] and the oppression of the White Man, as snow before a summer sun."

—Tecumseh, 1811

The U.S. general surrendered Detroit to the British. More American Indians joined Tecumseh's warriors after the British army's early successes.

At the beginning of the War of 1812 (1812–1814), Tecumseh's warriors and the British were successful. They won several battles. When they approached Detroit, Michigan, the U.S. general commanding the army in Detroit surrendered the town without a battle. British victories encouraged more American Indians to join Tecumseh's warriors.

But in August of 1812, a new general took charge of the British army in Michigan. This general did not respect Tecumseh's war skills and battle strategies. He also was not as forceful as the previous general had been. The British army and Tecumseh's warriors were not as successful under the new leadership.

Make a Water Drum

The Shawnee Indians used water drums during
ceremonies, at social dances, and before battles.

What You Need

empty, 13-ounce (368-gram) coffee can with lid

2 cups (500 mL) water

1 sheet brown construction paper, 12 inches by 18 inches
   (30.5 centimeters by 46 centimeters)

ruler

scissors

acrylic paints

paint brushes

tape

square piece of canvas, 10 inches by 10 inches
   (25 centimeters by 25 centimeters)

leather lace, 15 inches (38 centimeters) long

What You Do

1. Pour water into the coffee can. Securely place the lid on the can.

2. Cut the paper lengthwise with a 7-inch (18-centimeter) width.

3. Decorate the paper with painted designs.

4. Wrap the paper around the can, and secure it with tape.

5. Place the canvas over the top of the can.

6. Tie the leather lace around the canvas to hold the canvas piece in place.

7. Use your fingers to tap a rhythm on the canvas drum top.

CHAPTER 6

Death on the Thames

Tecumseh predicted his death at the Battle of the Thames.

After losing several battles against the American soldiers, Tecumseh's warriors became discouraged. Some of the American Indians returned to their villages. But Tecumseh stayed with the British army. He told his followers that fighting with the British was the only way the American Indian people could protect their way of life.

"When it comes your time to die, be not like those whose hearts are filled with fear of death, so that when their time comes they weep and pray for a little more time to live their lives over again in a different way. Sing your death song and die like a hero going home."

—*Tecumseh, 1812*

In early October 1813, Tecumseh, about 1,000 warriors, and the British army camped near the Thames River in Ontario, Canada. The group was being chased by the U.S. Army. Tecumseh convinced the British general to make a stand and battle the U.S. soldiers.

Tecumseh had a vision that he would be killed during the battle. He told the American Indian warriors about his vision. Tecumseh then passed out his personal weapons to his closest friends, keeping only his war club for himself.

To his closest friend, Tecumseh gave his rifle. He told his friend to stay close to him. "When I fall, touch my body with the tip of this gun four times," Tecumseh said. "I will rise and lead you to victory. If I do not rise, stop fighting and retreat."

On October 5, 1813, Tecumseh and his warriors fought the U.S. Army along the banks of the Thames River. Just as Tecumseh had predicted, a U.S. soldier shot and killed Tecumseh. When Tecumseh did not rise from the ground, his friend yelled, "Tecumseh's dead!" The warriors immediately retreated.

Great Britain lost the War of 1812 and its land claims in North America.

During the Battle of the Thames, a U.S. soldier shot and killed Tecumseh.

Tecumseh's Shawnee people and many other American Indian tribes were forced off their land and eventually onto reservations. On these government lands, the American Indians were not free to practice their traditional way of life. Today, many people remember Tecumseh for his vision of peace and freedom for the American Indian people.

Chronology

1775
Tecumseh's father dies in a battle with white soldiers.

1787
Chiksika dies during an attack on a U.S. fort.

1795
Some American Indian tribes sign a treaty with the United States, giving up claims to their northeastern lands.

October 5, 1813
Tecumseh dies in the Battle of the Thames.

1768
Tecumseh is born.

Fall 1810
Tecumseh travels south to gain the support of more American Indian tribes.

November 1811
The Prophet rallies warriors at Tippecanoe Village to fight U.S. soldiers. The warriors are defeated in the Battle of Tippecanoe.

1812
Tecumseh and his warriors join the British in the War of 1812.

Words to Know

ancestor (AN-sess-tur)—a member of a family or relation who lived long ago

compassion (kuhm-PASH-uhn)—a feeling of sympathy for someone and a desire to help someone

concentrate (KON-suhn-trate)—to focus your thoughts and attention on one object or activity

confederacy (kuhn-FED-ur-uh-see)—a union of people or tribes with a common goal

council (KOUN-suhl)—a meeting of a group of leaders chosen to look after the interests of a community

deliver (di-LIV-ur)—to help a baby be born

discouraged (diss-KUR-ijd)—feeling a lack of confidence

elder (EL-dur)—an older person; in American Indian tribes, an elder was an older, respected, and knowledgeable member of the village.

foretell (for-TEL)—to forecast or predict something

generosity (jen-u-ROSS-i-tee)—a quality of willingness to give to others

grieve (GREEV)—to feel very sad

strategy (STRAT-uh-jee)—a plan for winning a military battle or achieving a goal

surrender (suh-REN-dur)—to give up a fight or battle

traditional (truh-DISH-uhn-uhl)—having to do with the ways of the past

To Learn More

Flanagan, Alice K. *The Shawnee.* A True Book. New York: Children's Press, 1998.

Immell, Myra, and William H. Immell. *Tecumseh.* The Importance Of. San Diego: Lucent Books, 1997.

Mattern, Joanne. *The Shawnee Indians.* Native Peoples. Mankato, Minn.: Bridgestone Books, 2001.

Todd, Anne M. *The War of 1812.* America Goes to War. Mankato, Minn.: Capstone Books, 2001.

Internet Sites

Galafilm—War of 1812
http://www.galafilm.com/1812/e

Tecumseh!
http://www.tecumsehdrama.com

The Shawnee
http://www.merceronline.com/Native/native02.htm

To Be Shawnee
http://www.geocities.com/southbeach/cove/8286/child.html

Places to Visit

Ohio Historical Society
1982 Velma Avenue
Columbus, OH 43211

Tecumseh! Outdoor Drama
Sugarloaf Mountain Amphitheatre
5968 Marietta Road
Chillicothe, OH 45601

Tippecanoe Battlefield
200 Battle Ground Avenue
Battle Ground, IN 47920

Zane Shawnee Caverns
7092 State Route 540
Bellefontaine, OH 43311

Index